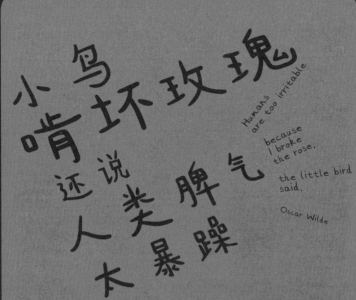

小鸟啃坏玫瑰
还说人类本暴躁脾气

Humans
are too irritable

because
I broke
the rose.

the little bird
said.

Oscar Wilde

〔英〕奥斯卡·王尔德 —— 著

刘露 —— 译

红花 —— 绘
HONGHUA

江苏凤凰文艺出版社

Oscar Wilde

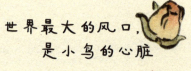

· 目

世界

最大的风口，

是

小鸟的

心脏

·毒舌小鸟·

小鸟
啃坏玫瑰
还说人类脾气
太暴躁

按自己的意愿生活，
不算自私；

要求他人
按自己的意愿生活，

才是自私。

小鸟
啃坏玫瑰
还说人类脾气
大暴躁

Selfishness
is not living as one wishes
to live,

it is asking others to live
as one wishes
to live.

世间百态，
毫无道理。

灾难
总以错误的方式，
发生在错误的对象身上。

喜剧
细思令人极恐，

悲剧
总以荒诞告终。

小鸟
啃坏玫瑰
还说人类脾气
大暴躁

For life
is terribly deficient
in form.
Its catastrophes happen in the wrong way
and to the wrong people.

There is a grotesque horror
about its comedies,
and its tragedies seem to culminate
in farce.

冷眼旁观
自己的生活，

便能逃离
生活的痛苦。

小鸟
啃坏玫瑰
还说人类脾气
大暴躁

To become the spectator
of one's own life,

is to escape the suffering
of life.

人以自己的身份说话时，

最
是
虚
伪。

给他一副面具，

他就会
告诉你真相。

小鸟
啃坏玫瑰
还说人类脾气
大暴躁

Man is least himself

when he talks in his own person.

Give him a mask,

and

he will tell you

the truth.

王尔德·经典短句集

同情
他人的感受，
多么容易。

理解
他人的想法，
那么困难。

小鸟
啃坏玫瑰
还说人类脾气
大暴躁

It is so easy
for people to have sympathy
with suffering.

It is so difficult
for them to have sympathy
with thought.

王尔德·经典妞句集

013

我们
总爱高看别人，
其实是在担心自己。

乐观的根源是恐惧。

我们赞美邻居，
自以为慷慨，
其实是因为，
我们希望别人的美德、
对我们有利。

The reason we all like to think so well
of others is that we are all afraid for
ourselves.

The basis of optimism is sheer terror.

We think
that we are generous
because we credit our neighbour
with the possession of those virtues that
are likely to be a benefit to us.

人做的

最蠢的事，

往往出于

最高尚的动机。

小鸟
啃坏玫瑰
还说人类脾气
大暴躁

Whenever a man does
a thoroughly stupid thing,

it is always from
the noblest motives.

世上
只有两种人
最迷人:

洞悉一切的人,
和
一无所知的人。

小鸟
啃坏玫瑰
还说人类脾气
大暴躁

There are
only two kinds of people
who are really fascinating—

people who know absolutely everything,
and
people who know absolutely nothing.

生活

向来不公……
但
对多数人而言,
或许是好事。

小鸟
啃坏玫瑰
还说人类脾气
大暴躁

Life

is never fair...
And perhaps
it is a good thing
for most of us that it is not.

我
太喜欢表演了,

比生活
真实多了。

小鸟
啃坏玫瑰
还说人类脾气
太暴躁

I love acting.

It is so much more real
than life.

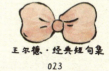

世界是个舞台，但

The world is a stage

小鸟
啃坏玫瑰
还说人类脾气
太暴躁

，出戏的选角太糟糕了。

ut the play is badly cast.

·毒舌小鸟·

我写作的时候，
还不懂生活；

如今

懂了生活，
便没什么可写的了。

生活
不该用来写作，

生活
该用来体验。

小鸟
啃坏玫瑰
还说人类脾气
大暴躁

I wrote
when I did not know life:

now

that I do know the meaning of life,
I have no more to write.

Life
cannot be written:

life
can only be lived.

纵使如何努力，
也无法透过现象看本质。

也许有个可怕的原因：

根本没有本质，
只有表面。

小鸟
啃坏玫瑰
还说人类脾气
太暴躁

Try as we may, we cannot get behind the appearance of things to reality.

And the terrible reason may be that there is no reality in the things apart from their appearances.

真正的奥秘
都不是虚无缥缈的，

而是实实在在的。

小鸟
啃坏玫瑰
还说人类脾气
大暴躁

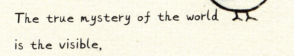

The true mystery of the world
is the visible,

not the invisible...

"诗意生活的人，

不仅用脑，

也用心。"

"不像那幅悲伤的画像，

有脸，

无心。"

小鸟
啃坏玫瑰
还说人类脾气
太暴躁

"If a man treats life artistically,
his brain
is his heart."

"Like the painting of a sorrow,
a face
without a heart."

如今这个时代,

书读得太多,
缺少智慧;
人想得太多,
失掉美感。

小鸟
啃坏玫瑰
还说人类脾气
太暴躁

We live in an age

that reads too much
to be wise,
and thinks too much
to be beautiful.

·毒舌小鸟·

找到
一个借口，

就能找到
千百个借口，

死性不改。

If you find one false excuse
for yourself,

you will soon find
a hundred,

and be just what you were before.

小鸟
啃坏玫瑰
还说人走脾气
太暴躁

每个人都把他的错误

Experience is the name everyone

小鸟
啃坏玫瑰
还说人类脾气
太暴躁

弥之 为经验。

ives to their mistakes.

经验这个东西不会激发行动，
如同良知一样。

经验真正说明的是：

未来会重蹈过去的覆辙——

我们一度嫌弃的那些错误，
日后仍会欣然重复犯下。

还说人类脾气太暴躁

There was no motive power in experience. It was as little of an active cause as conscience itself.

All that it really demonstrated was that our future would be the same as our past, and that the sin we had done once, and with loathing, we would do many times, and with joy.

可惜的是,
人往往在于事无补时,
才学会吸取教训.

小鸟
啃坏玫瑰
还说人类脾气
大暴躁

What a pity that in life
we only get our lessons
when they are of no use to us.

一个烧伤过的孩子
还是爱玩火。

小鸟
啃坏玫瑰
还说人类脾气
大暴躁

That a burnt child
loves the fire.

明智的决定
有一点很要命——

决定得

太晚。

小鸟
啃坏玫瑰
还说人类脾气
大暴躁

There is a fatality
about good resolutions—

that they are always made

too late.

你我现在如此，
将来也会如此，
本性难移。

至于书毒害人，
根本没有这样的事。

艺术不会激发行动，
只会让人不想行动，
劝退效果极好。

还说人类脾气大暴躁

You and I are what we are,

and

will be what we will be.

As for being poisoned by a book,

there is no such thing as that.

Art has no influence upon action.

It annihilates the desire to act.

It is superbly sterile.

销毁过去总是容易的，

悔恨、
否认、
遗忘，
都能做到，

但
未来
避无可避。

小鸟
啃坏玫瑰
还说人类脾气
大暴躁

The past could always be annihilated.

Regret,
denial,
or forgetfulness
could do that.

But
the future
was inevitable.

我从不
后悔过去，

经历
让我更了解自己。

小鸟
啃坏玫瑰
还说人类脾气
大暴躁

I am not sorry for anything
that has happened.

It has taught me
to know myself better.

每个圣人
都有过往，

每个罪人
都有未来。

小鸟
啃坏玫瑰
还说人类脾气
大暴躁

Every saint
has a past,

and every sinner
has a future.

我或许
不同意你的观点，

但我誓死捍卫
你愚蠢发言的权利。

小鸟
啃坏玫瑰
还说人类脾气
大暴躁

I may
disagree with you,

but I defend your right
to make a fool of yourself to the death.

王尔德·经典短句集

小鸟啃坏玫瑰

我不懂，
谁说人类是理性的动物。
这简直是
有史以来最草率的定义了。

人类有很多特点，
但理性绝对不在其列。

还说人类脾气大暴躁

I wonder who it was defined man
as a rational animal.
It was the most premature definition
ever given.

Man is many things,
but he is not rational.

这世上，
丑陋的人
和
愚蠢的人
最快活。

他们
虽然没尝过胜利的甜，
至少
也不懂失败的苦。

The ugly

and

the stupid

have the best of it

in this world.

If they know nothing

of victory,

they are at least spared the knowledge

of defeat.

想要"文明"，
可不容易。

只有两条路：

一条是修养，
另一条是堕落。

Civilization is not by any means an easy
thing to attain to.

There are only two ways by which man
can reach it.
One is by being cultured,
the other by being corrupt.

很少有人真正在生活.

多数人只是活着
而已.

小鸟
啃坏玫瑰
还说人类脾气
大暴躁

To live is the rarest thing in the world.

Most people exist,
that is all.

王尔德·经典短句集

我不想谋生，
我想好好生活。

小鸟
啃坏玫瑰
还说人类脾气
太暴躁

I don't want to earn a living,
I want to live.

生活不是投机,
而是圣礼。

人生的理想是爱,
它因牺牲而纯洁。

小鸟
啃坏玫瑰
还说人类脾气
太暴躁

It is not a speculation.
It is a sacrament.

Its ideal is love.
Its purification is sacrifice.

人生
或许只能拥有一次
伟大的体验，

而生活的秘诀在于，
多多重复那次体验。

小鸟
啃坏玫瑰
还说人类脾气
太暴躁

We can have in life
but one great experience
at best,

and the secret of life is to reproduce
that experience as often as possible.

支配生活的，
不是想法和意愿，

而是神经、纤维
逐渐生长的细胞所构筑的躯体，
里面藏着深邃的
思想
和
炽热的美梦。

还说人类脾气太暴躁

Life is not governed
by will or intention.

Life is a question of nerves, and fibres,
and
slowly built—up cells
in which thought hides itself
and
passion has its dreams.

真正的人生，

往往是
自己没有过上的那种。

小鸟
啃坏玫瑰
还说人类脾气
太暴躁

One's real life

is so often the life
that one does not lead.

现实生活凌乱不堪,

想象的生活却有一种
可怕的秩序感.

Actual life was chaos,

but there was something terribly logical
in the imagination.

据说，

大事都是在
脑海中发生的。

小鸟
啃坏玫瑰
还说人类脾气
太暴躁

It has been said

that the great events of the world
take place in the brain.

用

玫瑰

为自己

加冕

爱能读懂最遥远

Love can read the writin

小鸟
啃坏玫瑰
还说人类脾气
大暴躁

辰上的诗篇。

the remotest star.

世界上
任何牢笼，

爱
都能破门而入。

In any prison
in any world,

love
can break through the door.

小鸟
啃坏玫瑰
还说人类脾气
太暴躁

我那
风暴般的激情，
让我变得反常：

我的爱过于深沉，
成了无声的沉默。

So
my too stormy passions
work me wrong,

And for excess of love
my love is dumb.

那朵红玫瑰，
我会用月下的歌声铸就它，
再用我的心血染红它。

而我所求的，
不过是要你真挚地去爱。

小鸟
啃坏玫瑰
还说人类脾气
大暴躁

I will make it with a moonlit singing voice,
and I will dye it red
with my own pain's blood.

The only thing I want
from you is to be a true lover.

王尔德·经典组句集
089

"你爱他爱得很深吗？"

"真希望我能看清。"

"看清了就不爱了，看不清才有魅力。"

"Are you very much in love with him?"

"I wish I knew."

"Knowledge would be fatal. It is the uncertainty that charms one."

小鸟
啃坏玫瑰
还说人类脾气
太暴躁

我把灵魂全心全意交给你，
你却只当它是
夏日随手采下的一朵花，

别在衣服上，
满足虚荣。

小鸟
啃坏玫瑰
还说人类脾气
太暴躁

I have given away my whole soul to
someone who treats it as if it were a
flower to put in his coat,

a bit of decoration to charm his vanity,
an ornament for a summer's day.

你对人人都喜欢
You like everyone, that is to sa

小鸟
啃坏玫瑰
还说人类脾气
大暴躁

芒于对人人都漠然。

ou are indifferent to everyone.

当你不再爱这个人，

他的情感
就会显得

有些可笑了。

小鸟
啃坏玫瑰
还说人类脾气
大暴躁

There is always something ridiculous

about

the emotions of people

whom one has ceased to love.

·毒舌小鸟·

小鸟
啃坏玫瑰
还说人类脾气
太暴躁

"艺术是什么？"
"是一种疾病。"
"爱情呢？"
"是一种幻觉。"

"What of art?"
"It is a malady."
"Love?"
"An illusion."

如果
你真正爱上一个人，
眼里便再无他人。

爱能改变人。

小鸟
啃坏玫瑰
还说人类脾气
太暴躁

If one really loves a woman,
all other women in the world become
absolutely meaningless to one.

Love changes people.

啊!
若你对我,
少些欲望,
多些爱意,

在那些
欢笑与雨水交织的夏日后,
我便不会继承悲伤,
也不会屈从于痛苦。

还说人类脾气大暴躁

Ah!

Had'st thou liked me less

and

loved me more,

Through

all those summer days of joy and rain,

I had not now been sorrow's heritor,

or stood a lackey in the house of pain.

这个伤口，
被爱以外的任何东西触碰，
都会流血：

就算是爱，
也会让伤口流血，
但至少不痛。

小鸟
啃坏玫瑰
还说人类脾气
太暴躁

It is a wound that bleeds

when any hand

but

that of love touches it

and even then must bleed again,

though not for pain.

我知道，
花儿也有欲望，

玫瑰花瓣
也噙着泪水。

小鸟
啃坏玫瑰
还说人类脾气
太暴躁

I know that for me,
to whom flowers are part of desire,

there are tears waiting in
the petals of some rose.

小鸟啃坏玫瑰

人类以为，
情感可以随意产生，
毫无代价。

当然有代价，
即便是最高尚无私的情感，
也有代价。

还说人类脾气大暴躁

You think that one can
have one's emotions
for nothing.

One cannot.
Even the finest and the most self-
sacrificing emotions have to be paid for.

爱情不是商品，
不能论两称斤。
爱情的喜悦，
如同思维的喜悦，
在于感受自身的存在与活力。
爱情的目的就是去爱——
仅此而已，
不多不少。

还说人类脾气太暴躁

Love does not traffic in a marketplace,

nor use a huckster's scales.

Its joy,

like the joy of the intellect,

is to feel itself alive.

The aim of love is to love:

no more,

and no less.

人人都值得被爱，除

Everyone is worthy of love

小鸟
啃坏玫瑰
还说人类脾气
太暴躁

那些自以为值得的人。

xcept he who thinks that he is.

小鸟啃坏玫瑰

人人都会伤害心爱之人。
这一点人所共知。
有人用仇恨的眼神，
有人用谄媚的言语。
懦弱的人用亲吻，
勇敢的人用刀剑。

还说人类脾气太暴躁

And all men
kill the thing they love.
Some do it with a bitter look,
Some with a flattering word.
The coward does it with a kiss,
The brave man with a sword.

有人在青春时扼杀情愫，
有人在年迈时斩断情根。
有人出于欲望，
有人出于贪婪。
最仁慈的人用刀，
干脆利落。

有人爱得太少，有人爱得太多，
有人出卖爱情，有人购买爱情，
有人动手时泪流满面，
有人决绝得毫无哀叹。
人人都会伤害心爱之人，
却不一定因此遭受惩罚。

Some kill their love when they are young,
and some when they are old.
Some strangle with the hands of lust,
some with the hands of gold.
The kindest use a knife, because
the dead so soon grow cold.

Some love too little, some too long,
some sell and others buy,
some do the deed with many tears,
and some without a sigh.
For each man kills the thing he loves,
yet each man does not die.

·毒舌小鸟·

小鸟
啃坏玫瑰
还说人类脾气
太暴躁

爱情，
始于自我欺骗，
终于欺骗他人。

When one is in love,
one always begins by deceiving one's self,
and one always ends by deceiving others.

生活，
就是一件蠢事
赶着一件蠢事：

而爱情，
则是两个蠢货追来追去。

小鸟
啃坏玫瑰
还说人类脾气
太暴躁

Life is
one fool thing
after another

whereas love is
two fool things after each other.

小鸟
啃坏玫瑰
还说人类脾气
太暴躁

婚姻
真正的基础是

彼此
误解。

The proper basis

for marriage

is a mutual

misunderstanding.

一往情深，
是
无所事事之人的
特权。

小鸟
啃坏玫瑰
还说人类脾气
大暴躁

A grande passion
is
the privilege of people
who have nothing to do.

婚姻
不过是个坏习惯。

可是人会怀念习惯，
即使是最坏的习惯。

或许人最怀念的，
恰恰是这些坏习惯，
它们是人格中不可或缺的部分。

Married life
is merely a habit, a bad habit.

But then one regrets the loss
even of one's worst habits.

Perhaps one regrets them the most.
They are such an essential part of one's
personality.

爱已经不流行了，
诗人是罪魁祸首，
他们在诗篇里大肆歌颂爱，
如今都没人买账了，
一点不奇怪。

真正的爱是
痛苦的、
沉默的。

Love is not fashionable anymore,
the poets have killed it.
They wrote so much about it
that nobody believed them,
and I am not surprised.

True love
suffers,
and is silent.

浪漫

最糟糕的地方

在于，

让人变得如此不浪漫。

小鸟
啃坏玫瑰
还说人类娇气
大暴躁

The worst of having a romance
of any kind

is that

it leaves one so unromantic.

他们说，
爱是苦涩的……

但那又怎样？
我已经吻过你了。

小鸟
啃坏玫瑰
还说人类脾气
大暴躁

They say
that love is bitter...

But what dose it matter?
I already kissed you.

纵使懊悔——
青春那苍白的管家，
带着他所有的随从，
对我穷追不舍，

我仍然庆幸爱过你——
我思念，
让一株婆婆纳
变蓝的所有阳光！

Though remorse,
youth's white-faced seneschal,
tread on my heels
with all his retinue,

I am most glad I loved thee—
think of all
the suns that go to
make one speedwell blue!

浪漫永远不会死去，

就像月亮，
永远明亮。

Romance never dies.

It is like the moon,
and lives for ever.

小鸟
啃坏玫瑰
还说人类脾气
大暴躁

荆棘

也能成为

利剑

我们
都生活在阴沟里,

但

总有人

仰
望
星
空。

小鸟
啃坏玫瑰
还说人类脾气
大暴躁

We are
all in the gutter,

but

some of us

are looking at
the stars.

·毒舌小鸟·

小鸟
啃坏玫瑰
还说人类脾气
大暴躁

没有什么
比快乐更值得追寻,

没有什么
比幸福更容易流逝。

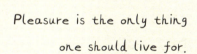

Pleasure is the only thing
one should live for.

Nothing ages
like happiness.

能后天再做的事，

我
绝不明天完成。

I never put off

till tomorrow

what I can possibly do — the day after.

小鸟
啃坏玫瑰
还说人类脾气
大暴躁

只有无趣之人
才会
在吃早餐时

展现
自己的才华。

小鸟
啃坏玫瑰
还说人走脾气
大暴躁

Only
dull people

are brilliant
at breakfast.

小鸟
啃坏玫瑰
还说人类脾气
太暴躁

谈论天气，

　　　　　是
无聊人类
最后的庇护所。

Conversation about the weather

　　　　　is

the last refuge

of the unimaginative.

我喜欢
简单的快乐，

那是
复杂之人
最后的避难所。

I adore
simple pleasures.

They are
the last refuge
of the complex.

小鸟
啃坏玫瑰
还说人类脾气
大暴躁

不要挥霍黄金岁月，
不要听从乏味说教，
不要试图扭转无望的失败，

不要为
无知、
平庸、
低俗之事

浪费生命。

Don't squander the gold of your days,
listening to the tedious,
trying to improve the hopeless failure,

or

giving away your life to
the ignorant,
the common,
and the vulgar.

青春到底是什么？

是一段青涩的时光，

多愁善感，
喜怒无常。

最好别念着过往，
毕竟无法改变。

小鸟
啃坏玫瑰
还说人类脾气
大暴躁

What was youth at best?

A green, an unripe time,

a time of shallow moods,
and sickly thoughts.

It was better not to think of the past.
Nothing could alter that.

不要垂头丧气，

即使

失去一切，
还有明天。

小鸟
啃坏玫瑰
还说人类脾气
太暴躁

Don't be discouraged

even if

you lose everything,
tomorrow will still be in your hands.

小鸟
啃坏玫瑰
还说人类脾气
大暴躁

一个人
想要重获青春，

重新
做以前的蠢事
就好了。

To get back
one's youth,

one has merely to
repeat
one's follies.

我唯一的错误，是只探索了世界这个大花园里阳光明媚的一面，忽略了阴暗忧郁的一面。我打定主意不去探索生活的阴暗面，反而被迫尝尽苦果。

我也曾尽情享乐：把灵魂的珍珠投入美酒，伴着笛声，迎着报春花翩翩起舞，啜饮蜜糖。

然而，
这样下去就错了，因为局限了生活的维度。

我需要突破。花园另一面也有它的秘密，等待我去探索。

My only mistake was that I confined myself so exclusively to the trees of what seemed to me the sun-lit side of the garden, and shunned the other side

for its shadow and its gloom.

And as I had determined to know nothing of them, I was forced to taste each one

of them in turn, to feed on them.

I threw the pearl of my soul into a cup of wine. I went down the primrose path to the sound of flutes. I lived on honeycomb. But to have continued the same life would have been wrong because it would have been limiting. I had to pass on. The other half of the garden had its secrets

for me also.

许多东西，
若不是怕别人捡去，
人们一定会丢弃。

小鸟
啃坏玫瑰
还说人类脾气
太暴躁

Many things will be thrown away
if they are not afraid of being picked up
by others.

比
被人议论更糟糕的，

是
没人议论。

小鸟
啃坏玫瑰
还说人类脾气
太暴躁

There is only one thing in the world worse
than being talked about,

and
that is not being talked about.

人生真正的悲剧都毫无美感，
简单粗暴，
这些苦难没有道理，
没有意义，
也没有品位，
只是纯粹地伤透你的心。

还说人类脾气大暴躁

It often happens that the real tragedies
of life occur in such an inartistic
manner that they hurt us by their crude
violence, their absolute incoherence,
their absurd want of meaning, their
entire lack of style.

· 毒舌小鸟 ·

别再愁眉苦脸啦！
永葆青春的秘诀，
就是别有坏情绪。

Don't look so tragic!
The secret of remaining young is never to
have an emotion that is unbecoming.

小鸟
啃坏玫瑰
还说人类脾气
大暴躁

不要期待
他人像自己一样优秀,

那样不公平。

小鸟
啃坏玫瑰
还说人类脾气
大暴躁

It would be unfair

to expect other people
to be as remarkable as oneself.

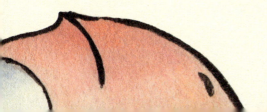

善良是
与自己和解,

纠结是
被迫迎合他人.

小鸟
啃坏玫瑰
还说人类脾气
大暴躁

To be good
is to be in harmony
with one's self.

Discord
is to be forced to be in harmony
with others.

想要影响一个人，

就得
给他

你的灵魂。

小鸟
啃坏玫瑰
还说人走脾气
大暴躁

To influence a person

is to give him
one's own

soul.

·毒舌小鸟·

如果
人活着只为自己,

怕是
要付出惨痛代价.

小鸟
啃坏玫瑰
还说人类脾气
大暴躁

If one lives merely
for one's self,

one pays a terrible price
for doing so.

我知道快乐是什么

I know what pleasure i

小鸟
啃坏玫瑰
还说人类脾气
大暴躁

快乐就是崇拜一个人。

t is to adore some one.

我
总想了解
新朋友的一切,

不关心
老朋友的
近况。

小鸟
啃坏玫瑰
还说人类脾气
大暴躁

I
always like to know everything
about my new friends,

and
nothing about
my old ones.

专程过来安慰我，
你人真好。

见我没那么难过了，
你又大发雷霆。

您可真有同情心啊！

小鸟
啃坏玫瑰
还说人类脾气
太暴躁

You come down here to console me.
That is charming of you.

You find me consoled,
and you are furious.

How like a sympathetic person!

任何人
都能同情朋友的不幸，

只有极其纯良之人
才能
庆贺朋友的成功。

小鸟
啃坏玫瑰
还说人太胖飞
太暴躁

Anybody can sympathise
with the sufferings of a friend,

but it requires a very fine nature
to sympathise
with a friend's success.

对于自己不在意的人，

我们
反而容易

释放

善
意。

One
can always be kind
to people
about
whom one cares nothing.

小鸟
啃坏玫瑰
还说人发脾气
太暴躁

王尔德·经典短句集

用笑声开始一段友谊，
一点也不赖；

用笑声结束一段友谊，
再好不过了。

小鸟
啃坏玫瑰
还说人类脾气
大暴躁

Laughter is not at all a bad beginning
for a friendship,

and it is far the best ending
for one.

欢笑背后，
也许是粗俗无礼、
冷酷无情。

但
悲伤背后，
向来只有悲伤。

痛苦与欢乐不一样，
从不伪装。

Behind joy and laughter
there may be a temperament,
coarse, hard and callous.

But
behind sorrow
there is always sorrow.

Pain, unlike pleasure,
wears no mask.

曾经的生活多么美好，
如今却在这废墟上，

痛苦崩溃，
害怕茫然，
心力交瘁。

但是我不想恨你了。

每天我都告诉自己：
"今天心中也要有爱呀，不然
可怎么熬过来呢！"

还说人类脾气太暴躁

I sat admist the ruins
of my wonderful life,

crushed by anguish,
bewildered with terror,
dazed through pain.

But I would not hate you.

Every day I said to myself:
"I must keep love in my heart today,
else how shall I live through the day."

令人震撼的

不是
苦难的神秘之处,

而是
苦难的荒诞可笑——

那般无用,
那般缺乏意义。

小鸟
啃坏玫瑰
还说人类脾气
大暴躁

And yet it was not the mystery,

but the comedy of suffering
that struck him:

its
absolute uselessness,

its
grotesque want of meaning.

痛苦是漫长的时刻，
无法划分为季节，
只能记录它的阴晴不定、
反复无常。

时间仿佛不再向前，
而在旋转，
围着痛苦打转。

Suffering is one long moment.
We cannot divide it by seasons.
We can only record its moods,
and chronicle their return.

With us time itself does not progress.
It revolves. It seems to circle round one
centre of pain.

不管
事情有多么糟糕,

知道真相,

也总比
这该死的悬而未决
来得好。

小鸟
啃坏玫瑰
还说人类脾气
太暴躁

It was better
to know the worst,
whatever it was,

than
to be left
in this hideous uncertainty.

我那高级的品位，
才是
我过得如此糟糕的理由。

小鸟
啃坏玫瑰
还说人类脾气
太暴躁

Good taste is the excuse
I've always given for leading
such a bad life.

人
到了该懂事的年纪，

反而
什么也不懂了。

小鸟
啃坏玫瑰
还说人类脾气
太暴躁

As soon as people
are old enough to know better,

they
don't know anything at all.

人生的目的
是成长。

将天性
发挥到极致,

是
我们来这世上的
目的。

小鸟
啃坏玫瑰
还说人类脾气
大暴躁

The aim of life
is self-development.

To realize
one's nature
perfectly—

that is what each of us
is here for.

不再成长的人生

No life is spoiled but on

小鸟
啃坏玫瑰
还说人类脾气
大暴躁

十算是毁了。

hose growth is arrested.

一个人，
可能常常虚度，
碌碌无为，
也可能
一朝际遇纷至沓来。

小鸟
啃坏玫瑰
还说人类脾气
太暴躁

One
can live for years
sometimes without living at all,
and then all life comes crowding
into one single hour.

爱

是

人类唯一的

救赎

爱自己，是终身

To love oneself is the beginnin

小鸟
啃坏玫瑰
还说人发脾气
大暴躁

良漫的开始.

f a lifelong romance.

·毒舌小鸟·

当我们
快乐时，
我们总能善良；

当我们
善良时，
却不一定快乐。

When

we are happy,

we are always good.

but

when we are good,

we are not always happy.

小鸟
啃坏玫瑰
还说人类脾气
大暴躁

·蒙古小鸟·

小鸟
啃坏玫瑰
还说人类脾气
大暴躁

人总爱劝诫他人，

而最需要这些建议的
恰恰是自己。

真是慷慨至极啊！

People are very fond of giving away

what they need most
themselves.

It is what I call the depth of generosity.

为了自己，
我必须宽恕你。

人不能
总是心怀怨念，
像有条毒蛇
缠绕心田；

也不能夜夜起身，
在灵魂的花园里种满荆棘。

For my own sake,
I must forgive you.

One cannot
always keep an adder
in one's breast
to feed on one,

nor rise up every night to sow thorns
in the garden of one's soul.

我的心
偷偷返回
那荒度千年的岁月，

呼唤那个
徘徊在苍茫海边的孤勇者，

他在
徒然地
寻找一个安身立命之所。

还说人类脾气太暴躁

My heart

stole back

across wide wastes of years.

To one

who wandered by a lonely sea,

and

sought in vain

for any place of rest.

狐狸有洞，
小鸟有巢，

而我，
只有我，
不得不疲惫漂泊，
迈开淤伤的双脚，
饮下泪浸的苦酒。

小鸟
啃坏玫瑰
还说人类脾气
大暴躁

Foxes have holes,
and every bird its nest,

I,
only I,
must wander wearily,
and bruise my feet,
and drink wine salt with tears.

没有什么
比人类遭受的苦难
更了不起,

苦难
是最伟大的奥秘。

小鸟
啃坏玫瑰
还说人类脾气
大暴躁

More marvelous
than anything
is the suffering of men and women.

There is no mystery so great
as misery.

·毒舌小鸟·

小鸟
啃坏玫瑰
还说人类脾气
大暴躁

奇怪的是，
不曾有人告诉我，
头脑这方寸之地，

竟
容得下

天堂
与
地狱。

Strange
that I was not told
that the brain can hold

In
a tiny ivory cell

God's heaven
and
hell.

世上只有两种悲剧：

一种是
得不到自己想要的，

另一种是
得到了。

小鸟
啃坏玫瑰
还说人类脾气
大暴躁

In this world there are only two tragedies.

One
is not getting what one wants,

and the other
is getting it.

王尔德·经典妞句集

小鸟
啃坏玫瑰
还说人类脾气
太暴躁

上天
想要惩罚我们时，

便会
回应我们的祈祷。

When
the gods wish to punish us,

they answer
our prayers.

我知道，
你有你的脆弱，
就像塑像的泥足。

谁能比我更清楚呢？

正是这脆弱，
才使塑像的金身格外珍贵。

还说人类脾气太暴躁

I knew
you had feet
of clay.

Who knew it better?

It was simply the feet of clay
that made the gold of the image precious.

亲爱的，已经无话可说

Sweet, there is nothing left to

小鸟
啃坏玫瑰
还说人发脾气
太暴躁

剩下的无非是：爱不会消逝。

say. But this, that love is never lost.

王尔德·经典短句集

你洞悉一切，
而我
一无所知。

但我相信，
人生不会虚度，

我知道，
我们终会重逢，
在某个永恒的瞬间。

还说人类脾气大暴躁

Thou knowest all—

I

cannot see.

I trust

I shall not live in vain,

I know

that we shall meet again

In some divine eternity.

· 垂古小鸟 ·

我们的生命之花
已被真理的蛀虫吞噬，

没有一只手
能拾起
青春凋零的
玫瑰花瓣。

For the crimson flower of our life
is eaten by the cankerworm of truth,

and no hand
can gather up
the fallen withered petals of the rose
of youth.

小鸟
啃坏玫瑰
还说人类脾气
大暴躁

不用说，
我的任务还没完成。
要能完成就好了。

前路漫漫，
还有更陡峭的山峰要攀登，
更黑暗的山谷要穿越。

只能靠自己，
宗教、道德、理性，
一概帮不上忙。

I need not say

that my task does not end there.

It would be comparatively easy if it did.

There is much more before me.

I have hills far steeper to climb,

valleys much darker to pass through.

And I have to get it all out of myself.

Neither religion, morality,

nor reason can help me at all.

"唉！"
我叹息道，

"我的生命充满痛苦，
这田野荒芜，无边无际，
要怎么收获果实和麦穗？"

我的渔网破败不堪，
但我仍孤注一掷，
把它撒向大海，
等待最后的结局。

还说人类脾气大暴躁

"Alas!"
I cried,

"my life is full of pain, and who can
garner fruit or golden grain, from these
waste fields which travail ceaselessly!"

My nets gaped wide with many a break
and flaw, nathless I threw them as my
final cast into the sea,
and waited for the end.

我知道,
如果选择恨你,

那么
本就如同在沙漠跋涉的我,
会难上加难,

日子昏天黑地,
草木枯萎,
连饮水
都苦涩不堪。

小鸟
啃坏玫瑰
还说人类脾气
大暴躁

I knew,

if I allowed myself to hate you,

that in the dry desert of existence over

which I had to travel,

and am travelling still,

every rock would lose its shadow,

every palm tree be withered,

every well of water prove poisoned at

its source.

我有别人无法掠夺的财富

I do possess what none can take awa

小鸟
啃坏玫瑰
还说人类牌气
太暴躁

爱，和所有星辰的荣光。

y love, and all the glory of the stars.

快乐
属于美好的肉体，

痛苦
属于美丽的灵魂。

Pleasure

for the beautiful body,

but pain

for the beautiful soul.

小鸟
啃坏玫瑰
还说人类脾气
大暴躁

唯有感官
能治愈灵魂,

就像

唯有灵魂
能治愈感官。

Nothing can cure the soul
but the senses,

just as

nothing can cure the senses
but the soul.

用灵魂
去生活,

就会
单纯得像个孩子。

When one comes in contact
with the soul,

it makes one simple
as a child.

小鸟
啃坏玫瑰
还说人类脾气
大暴躁

最可怕的
不是心碎——
心本就会碎——

而是
变得心如铁石。

小鸟
啃坏玫瑰
还说人类脾气
大暴躁

The most terrible thing about it
is not that it breaks one's heart—
hearts are made to be broken—

but

that it turns one's heart to stone.

情感的魔力
在于，
会引人误入歧途：

科学的好处
在于，
不受情感摆布。

小鸟
啃坏玫瑰
还说人类脾气
太暴躁

The advantage
of the emotions
is that they lead us astray,

and the advantage
of science
is that it is not emotional.

绝对肯定的事情,
往往
都不是真相。

这是
信仰带来的弊端,
也是
浪漫给人的教训。

The things
one feels absolutely certain about
are never true.

That is
the fatality of faith,
and
the lesson of romance.

悔恨过去，
等于停止成长。

否认过往，
等于
对人生撒谎，
不亚于
否认自己的灵魂。

还说人类脾气太暴躁

To regret one's own experiences
is to arrest one's own development.

To deny one's own experiences
is to put a lie
into the lips of one's own life.
It is no less
than a denial of the soul.

"我给出的
是
明天的真理。"

"但
我更喜欢
今天的错误。"

小鸟
啃坏玫瑰
还说人发脾气
太暴躁

"I give the truths
of
tomorrow."

"I prefer the mistakes
of
today."

甜蜜的回忆里，
也有苦涩；

愉悦的记忆里，
也有痛苦。

创造这样的世界，
似乎
才是人生的意义。

小鸟
啃坏玫瑰
还说人类脾气
大暴躁

The remembrance even of joy

having its bitterness

and the memories of pleasure

their pain.

It was the creation of such worlds

as these that seemed

to be the true object.

多数人活着，
是为了得到

爱
和
赞美；

其实是因为爱和赞美，
我们才活得下去。

Most people

live for

love

and

admiration.

But it is by love and admiration

that we should live.

不真诚
很危险,

但

过分真诚
足以致命.

小鸟
啃坏玫瑰
还说人类脾气
太暴躁

Not being sincere
is dangerous,

and

being too sincere
is absolutely fatal.

王尔德·经典短句集
269

世上唯一
可怕的

是厌倦,

这是
唯一无法宽恕的罪责。

小鸟
啃坏玫瑰
还说人类脾气
大暴躁

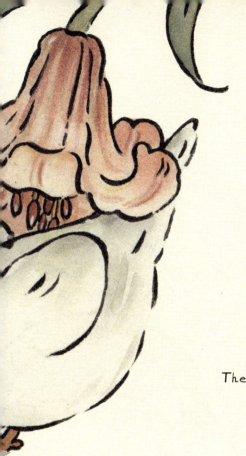

The only horrible thing
in the world

is ennui.

That is the one sin for which there
is no forgiveness.

摆脱诱惑的唯一办法，

就是
臣服于诱惑……

我什么都能抵挡，

除
了
诱
惑。

小鸟
啃坏玫瑰
还说人类脾气
大暴躁

The only way to get rid of temptation

is

to yield to it...

I can resist everything

but

temptation.

我认为，

美

是最神奇的东西，

只有肤浅的人
才不以貌取人。

小鸟
骂坏玫瑰
还说人类脾气
大暴躁

To me,

beauty

is the wonder of wonders.

It is only shallow people
who do not judge by appearances.

人

怎么能以好坏
来区分呢?

人,

要么
光芒四溢,

要么
平淡无奇。

小鸟
啃坏玫瑰
还说人变脾气
大暴躁

It is absurd to divide people

into
good and bad.

People are

either

charming

or

tedious.

王尔德·经典短句集

"所有的路，
都通往同一个终点。"

"是什么？"

"幻灭。"

"那是我人生的起点。"

还说人类脾气大暴躁

"All ways
end at the same point."

"What is that?"

"Disillusion."

"It was my debut in life."

自由、
书籍、
花朵、
月亮，

有了这些，
还有谁会不开心呢？

小鸟
啃坏玫瑰
还说人类脾气
太暴躁

With

freedom,

books,

flowers,

and the moon,

who could not be happy?

你所爱的地方

Any place you lov

小鸟
啃坏玫瑰
还说人类脾气
大暴躁

……是你的全世界。

…… the world to you.

Humans
are too irritable
because
I broke
the rose,
the little bird
said.

Oscar Wilde   Design *by* Yoshioka_Yuutarou in 2024.